My Magical Pony

Bright Eyes

The **My Magical Pony** series:

Other series by Jenny Oldfield:

Definitely Daisy
Totally Tom
The Wilde Family
Horses of Half Moon Ranch
My Little Life
Home Farm Twins

Bright Eyes

By Jenny Oldfield

Illustrated by Alasdair Bright

Hodder
Children's
Books

A division of Hodder Headline Limited

Chapter One

"Stand!" Krista told Misty.

She picked up the limping pony's front hoof and carefully scraped out some dried mud and a small, sharp stone.

"There!" Krista spotted the stone as it landed on the stable floor. She let go of the hoof. "That's what gave you the problem!"

Nervously Misty tested her weight on the sore foot.

Krista grinned as she slipped the hoof-pick into her jeans pocket. "See!" she murmured. "No more nasty stone to make you limp."

My Magical Pony

The pony stood firm and nuzzled Krista's shoulder as if to say thanks. Then she nosed in the corner of her stable for food.

"Hey, it's not feed time!" Krista laughed. "I only brought you inside to fix that foot."

"Did you sort it?" Jo asked, passing the stable door with a bale of straw. Jo Weston owned the stables.

Krista bent to pick up the sharp stone and show it to Jo. "Problem solved. Shall I put Misty back out in her field?"

"Yes please. But watch out for cars – I'm expecting visitors any minute."

So Krista led Misty out into the early autumn sun, checking that the pony was walking soundly as they crossed the yard into the lane. She stood to one side as a silver car drove in through the gate.

I know that kid! she said to herself, catching sight of the passenger in the car. It was a girl with long, straight, reddish brown hair, her face half hidden beneath a long,  thick fringe. "That's the new girl at school," she told Misty.

The pony lowered her head and nuzzled Krista's shirt pocket.

My Magical Pony

"I mean 'new', as in just arrived at the start of last week. Her name's Alice." Chattering on as she led the pony up the lane, Krista let her in on a secret. "Don't tell anyone, Misty, but I don't really like her."

The little grey nipped the edge of Krista's pocket between her front teeth.

"Hey, don't tear it!" she laughed. "No, I don't have any Polos in there, honest! Anyway, listen. Alice Henderson has moved in to a house on our lane. You'd think she'd want to be friends. But when I tried to talk to her on the way home from school on Tuesday, she blanked me."

Krista and Misty had reached the gate to the middle field. The pony pulled

sideways, trying to get at the juicy grass
growing by the roadside.

"And you know what – she never smiles or
laughs. She just sits in lessons looking dead
miserable." Krista sighed. "Hey, I sound mean,
talking about Alice like that, don't I?"

Misty raised her head and seemed to nod.

Krista laughed. "Yeah, sorry! I won't go on about it." Fishing in her back pocket for her hidden packet of mints, Krista gave one to the pony, who crunched it and licked her lips.

I guess moving schools isn't much fun, Krista thought. She headed back to the yard to finish her chores for the afternoon. *I wouldn't like it because I wouldn't have any friends. And even worse — I'd have to say goodbye to Misty and all the others here at Hartfell.*

No ponies! The idea made Krista shudder. She lived for ponies — they meant everything to her.

"Good news, Krista!" Jo called her across. "Alice is going to start riding with us here at Hartfell. You two know each other, don't you?"

Bright Eyes

Krista made a big effort to be nice. She grinned at the new girl. "Yeah, we're in the same class. Hi, Alice."

Alice kept her head down and didn't reply.

"She's shy," her mum said hastily. "Listen, Jo, Alice has done quite a bit of riding. She used to help out at a stable yard near to our old house in Scotland. The owner let her ride the ponies in her spare time."

"Cool!" Krista tried again. "Jo lets me do that too. We could ride down to the beach together, once you get used to things here."

It was no good. Alice kept her face hidden by her thick hair, refusing to be drawn in.

This time her mum sighed. "I'm hoping the riding will bring her out of her shell," she told Jo, taking her to one side. "Since we came down to Whitton, her dad and I hardly recognise her as the happy-go-lucky girl we were used to."

"It's hard for kids of her age to start again," Jo agreed. The two women walked and talked, leaving Krista to cope with a silent Alice.

"Do you want to come and see the horses in the bottom field?" Krista asked. "We've got two Welsh cobs and Apollo, who's a grey thoroughbred. He's Jo's horse."

Alice frowned and shook her head.

"Come on. He's really cool."

At last Alice looked up. "I said no!" she told Krista angrily. And before Krista could react, she stormed off across the yard.

Bright Eyes

"That kid's having a hard time," Jo said with a shake of her head.

It was five minutes since Mrs Henderson had driven off with her daughter, but until now both Krista and the owner of Hartfell stables had been lost in their own thoughts.

What did I say? Krista had asked herself.

How come Alice was so angry with me? "She nearly bit my head off," she told Jo.

"Yeah, but it's not your fault," Jo assured her. "You did your best to make her feel at home."

"It must be tough, being the new kid." Krista helped Jo cut the string on a bale of straw and scatter it in Apollo's stable. *Maybe I can help,* she thought, suddenly struck by a fresh and exciting idea. Quickly she spread the straw and made for the door.

"Where are you off to?" Jo yelled after her.

Krista didn't stop. "Sorry, I've gotta go!" she called.

"See you tomorrow?"

"Yep. Bye!"

Bright Eyes

"Bye." Following her to the door, Jo stared after Krista. She watched her grab her bike from outside the tack-room door and pedal off across the yard. *What got into her?* she wondered, going back to spread another bale of straw.

There was one pony in Krista's life who she never told anyone about.

I've got to find Shining Star! she said to herself, pedalling hard up the cliff path. *I need to talk to him about Alice Henderson!*

Shining Star had a long white mane and tail, his silver grey coat shimmered and glowed.

Star will sort out Alice's problems, Krista thought. *He always comes to help kids in trouble!*

My Magical Pony

Her secret pony was special. He had
magic powers, he appeared out of nowhere in
a glittering silver cloud.

Krista could hardly wait to see Shining
Star again. She cycled so hard to the top of
the cliff that her legs ached. At last she
reached the magic spot.

The wind blew fresh and salty off the sea.
Way below, the beach of Whitton Bay was a
narrow golden strip edged by curling white
waves.

This was the place where the magical pony
always appeared. Krista gazed up into the
clear sky, looking for a sign.

"I'm here!" she said out loud. "Shining Star,
where are you?"

Bright Eyes

The breeze lifted her wavy dark hair from her face and rippled through the green ferns that grew on the side of Hartfell.

"I need to talk to you about helping someone!" Krista called out. "There's a new

girl called Alice. She's just moved here and
she won't speak to anyone. Something is
really bugging her!"

For a moment she thought she saw a light,
wispy cloud soar over the ridge of Hartfell –
a signal that Shining Star was on his way.

Krista pictured the whirl of silvery mist,
the loud beating of wings.

But then two walkers appeared on the path
and the wisp of cloud vanished. The man and
the woman trudged towards the magic spot in
bright orange jackets, heavy rucksacks on
their backs.

Oops! Krista was sure that they'd heard her
talking to thin air.

The woman gave her a strange look before

she took off her rucksack and set it on the ground. "How about stopping here for tea?" she asked the man, getting out a thermos flask.

So that was it. As the couple sat down on the magic spot, Krista shrugged and picked up her bike. Maybe Jo was right – the Hendersons would have to sort out their own problems.

Krista free-wheeled down the hill.

OK, Shining Star, I'll see you another time! she thought, glancing wistfully at the vast, empty sky.

When you really need me, a wise voice seemed to reply, *I'll be here, ready and waiting!*

Chapter Two

"She talks funny," Carrie Jordan whispered to her friend, Holly Owen. They were huddled in a corner of the classroom, gossiping about new girl Alice.

"*Does* she talk?" Holly giggled. "That's news to me!"

"Yeah, her voice is weird," Carrie insisted, only shutting up when their teacher, Mrs Banks, glared at them.

Krista felt herself go red. She was sitting next to Alice, and she'd heard every word. It wasn't as if Krista had been joining in the gossip, but she still felt bad for the new girl.

Meanwhile Alice stared blankly at the book she was supposed to be reading.

Poor kid, Krista thought. Alice still didn't have any friends, though she'd been in school for two whole weeks. Instead of joining in, she spent her playtimes alone, hanging about by the gate, looking like she'd rather be anywhere than Whitton Junior. During lessons, she rarely looked up from her desk.

Her face is kind of blank, Krista thought. *You can never tell what she's thinking.*

Yet Alice had a pretty face, with unusual greyish-green eyes. The eyes, though, were as dull and blank as the rest of her features.

"Krista?" Mrs Banks broke into Krista's

thoughts. "It's not like you to be daydreaming. Didn't you hear what I said?"

"Sorry, miss – no, I didn't." Krista's blush deepened.

"I asked you to show Alice where we keep the PE equipment. I want you two to set it out in the hall after break."

So Krista took Alice to the store behind the assembly hall. She just had time to show her the PE mats and benches before the playtime bell rang.

"Come and practise netball in the yard," Krista suggested, hoping that for once Alice wouldn't have to hang about by herself.

But Alice shook her head.

Krista didn't let it drop. "Come on!

Bright Eyes

You shouldn't take any notice of Carrie and Holly, y'know."

Alice flashed her an angry look. "You don't have to talk to me!" she retorted.

"I don't ... I mean ... that's not ..." Krista stammered.

"I don't want you trying to be my friend just because you feel sorry for me!" Tears had sprung up in Alice's green eyes, and she rushed off down the crowded corridor towards the girls' toilets before Krista could protest.

"Weird!" Holly laughed, as she and Carrie strolled by.

Krista ignored them and on the spur of the moment decided to follow Alice.

Inside the washroom she found one of the cubicle doors locked and the sound of sobbing coming from the other side.

"Alice?" Krista knocked nervously on the door.

The sobs stopped.

"Alice, it's me – Krista."

Silence from inside the cubicle.

"Listen, I'm trying to help here. Only, there's nothing I can do unless you tell me what's wrong."

Bright Eyes

Still silence.

"Anyway, whatever it is, there's no need to take it out on me!" Krista said, suddenly feeling peeved.

There was a pause, then the bolt slid back and Alice opened the door. "Sorry," she murmured.

Wow! Krista hadn't expected the apology. "It's OK," she mumbled back.

Alice sniffed and pushed her hair behind her ears. Her eyes were red. "I want to go back home to Scotland," she confessed. "I can't stop thinking about it."

"Right." Krista nodded. Now that Alice had started to open up, she hoped that nobody would come barging into the cloakroom.

"You're homesick," she said. "It must be really hard."

Alice nodded. "We left my gran up in Scotland," she told Krista. "She's not well."

"That's tough."

"And I used to ride a pony called Nessie. That wasn't her real name, but she could be a little terror, so I nicknamed her after the Loch Ness monster."

Krista smiled. She and Alice really did have something in common – ponies! "What colour is Nessie?"

"Grey, like Misty. She's seven. She didn't actually belong to me, so I had to leave her behind. I miss her so much!"

"*Really* tough!" Krista said. She found

she was almost in tears herself.

When the bell went for the end of playtime both Krista and Alice had to reach for the paper towels and blow their noses hard.

"C'mon, we have to set up for PE," Krista told Alice, holding the cloakroom door open.

Hanging her head, Alice went ahead of Krista down the corridor. "Thanks," she said quietly.

"That's OK," Krista murmured. But she knew it wasn't OK for poor Alice, or her sick gran, or for lonely little Nessie who had lost a friend who loved her.

Next day was Saturday and Krista told her mum that she wanted to get to the stables early.

"I promised Alice that I'd school Misty before the ten o'clock hack so that Alice can ride her."

"Ah, Alice!" Krista's mum smiled. "Did you two finally make friends?"

"Sort of." Krista was in a rush to feed Spike, her pet hedgehog, but her mum said she would do it before she went shopping.

"Did you brush your teeth?" Krista's dad reminded her.

"Did you make your bed?" her mum asked.

"Yes! Yes!" Krista was out of the door and on her bike before they had time to fire any more questions at her.

Deciding to cycle along the lanes rather than take the cliff path, she whizzed down

Bright Eyes

the hill past the Hendersons' stone cottage,
then swung left along Mill Lane, up St
Michael's Hill and out on to the track leading
up to Hartfell stables. She arrived there
before nine, and by a quarter past had Misty
tacked up and out in the arena.

"OK, Misty, you're going to have a new

rider today," Krista said as she trotted the grey pony in a figure of eight. "I want you to be extra specially nice to her because she's not feeling great. You can show her that it's not all bad living here!"

The proud little pony launched into a smooth extended trot, head high, tail swishing.

"Cool!" Krista grinned. If a ride to the beach on Misty didn't cheer Alice up, then nothing would.

OK, so Krista had known it wouldn't be easy.

She took one look at Alice's pale, miserable face and dull eyes and saw just *how* hard it would be.

Mrs Henderson had dropped her off at

the gate, and Alice was frowning as she crossed the yard.

"Hi, Alice. You're just in time," Jo called, ready to take Apollo out at the head of a group of six riders.

Krista held Misty's reins as Alice mounted. Alice nodded but didn't speak.

Then Krista ran to fetch Drifter from his stable. They were the last to leave the yard, so Krista swung the gate closed, then caught up with Alice. "You look great on Misty," she said brightly. "She really suits you!"

Alice's frown deepened. "Leave me alone," she mumbled.

Krista shrugged. It seemed they were back to square one.

My Magical Pony

How can she not be enjoying this? Krista wondered as Jo led the group of riders through the ferns, down towards the beach. It was a great autumn day – the hills were green and golden brown, the sea glittered in the sunlight. As for the ponies, they were loving every minute.

"Be ready to canter when we get to the beach," Krista told Alice, sneaking a glance at the new girl's face. "Misty's got a brilliant canter, you'll see!"

And sure enough, the grey pony seemed to want to impress. The minute her hooves hit the firm sand, she threw herself into a joyful lope.

Alice sat easily in the saddle and gave the pony her head. Misty quickly overtook three other riders and caught up with Apollo. Krista and Drifter were close on their heels.

"Good rider!" Jo said to Krista as she let Alice and Misty pull ahead.

Misty was already galloping through the shallow waves, sending up a white spray.

Alice rode fearlessly and fast.

"No, make that *excellent* rider!" Jo corrected herself. "The girl's a natural!"

Krista grinned and urged Drifter to catch up with Alice. They were almost neck and neck when they reached the rocky headland.

For a moment Krista saw that Alice's face had come alive – her eyes were bright with excitement, shining with fun.

"Whoa, Nessie!" Alice cried, reining her pony back from the rocks.

Krista heard the slip of the tongue and gasped. She saw Alice blink.

"Alice—" Krista began.

But Alice cut her short. "I told you to leave me alone!" she snapped. "Why are you hanging around me all the time?"

"I'm not ... I didn't ..." Krista reined
Drifter back.

"Don't you understand – I don't want you
to be my friend!" Alice insisted, her voice
rising above the breaking waves. "I don't need
you! All I want is to go home!"

Chapter Three

"It's so hard!" Krista sighed. She was with Spike in the back garden at High Point Farm after another long day at the stables.

"I mean, it's like a smack in the face. I'm only trying to be nice, and then, whack! Alice tells me to go away and leave her alone."

The little hedgehog ambled easily across the lawn. Evening was a great time for him, especially now that the leaves had begun to turn brown and fall from the trees. He liked to snuffle amongst them for hidden slugs and creepy crawlies.

Bright Eyes

Krista lay back, her arms behind her head, staring up at the pearl-grey sky. "It makes me feel like I won't bother to be her friend any more," she grumbled.

She was still gazing up at the shifting clouds when her mum came out of the house carrying a plastic container.

"How do you fancy blackberry crumble for pudding tonight?" she asked.

"Yum!" Krista said.

Her mum grinned and gave her the carton. "So all we need are the blackberries!"

"Fine by me!" Krista agreed, scrambling up. "I've seen some great bushes on the cliff path. They're loaded with fruit."

*

My Magical Pony

Ten minutes later, she was picking the juicy
purple berries.

*How come the best ones are always just out of
reach?* she wondered, stretching as far as she
could. "Ouch!" She scratched her hand on the
prickles and retreated on to the path.

She was still sucking her sore finger when
a warm wind suddenly got up. There was a
flap of wings and a mist sweeping down from
the sky, soon surrounding Krista.

"Shining Star!" she gasped.

The mist clung to her, covering her in
silvery droplets, dampening her face as she
looked up to greet her magical pony.

"I'm on the magic spot!" she realised,
searching in the mist for those beautiful

dark eyes and fine, flowing mane.

Gradually Shining Star appeared, more gorgeous even than Krista remembered, with his silvery smooth coat that glittered and glistened, his strong, arched neck and fine, pricked ears.

"Are the berries good?" he asked, in his wise, gentle voice. He folded his wide wings against his sides.

She nodded. "Mum wants them for supper. I didn't know you were coming."

"You called for me before, but I could not appear."

Krista remembered the two hikers and nodded.

"Besides, I have been busy," Shining Star

My Magical Pony

told her. "There is much to do in Galishe."

"Where is Galishe?" Krista asked. Her magical pony would talk of the place where he came from, but she knew little about it.

"It is beyond the stars," he replied mysteriously.

"And the other creatures – are they all beautiful and silvery, like you?"

"Galishe glitters. All who live there glow with a silver light."

Krista's eyes were wide and shiny. "I wish I could go there with you!"

"It is wonderful," Star told her, leaning his head close to hers and allowing her to stroke his neck. "But tell me now about this child with the long red hair and the sad eyes."

"Alice!" Krista marvelled how Shining Star could know about a problem before she'd even told him. It was as if he could read her mind. "She's very unhappy."

Shining Star nodded. "She is pining for the place she loves."

"Yes, she's homesick for Scotland," Krista agreed. "I want to help, but Alice won't let me, and then I thought of you!"

Star's eyes looked intently into Krista's. "Tell me your plan."

She took a deep breath. "Scotland is a long way away," she began. "It takes hours and hours to get there. But I was thinking how much happier Alice would be if she could just whizz back and see everything

– her gran, her old house, Nessie …"

"Nessie?" Star interrupted.

"The pony she had to leave behind. If you could use your magic to fly Alice to her old home, how cool would that be!"

The magical pony listened carefully. "You believe that would bring the light back into the girl's eyes?" he asked.

Krista nodded. "If she could just check that her gran was OK, and if she could stroke Nessie, and maybe even ride her along the shore of the loch …" Krista recalled how Alice had ridden Misty along Whitton Sands, thinking for one exciting moment that she was on Nessie and they were galloping together.

"Then her eyes would sparkle again?"

"They would!" Krista insisted. "Shining Star, can you do it?"

The pony shook his head. "Your plan is kindly meant," he told her. "But remember that I am *your* magical pony. I cannot reveal my powers to anyone else."

Krista frowned. "Couldn't you fly Alice to Scotland and fly her back again, then make her forget how it had all happened?"

"No," Star said gently but firmly. "I cannot trick the people who I am sent to help. But perhaps there is another way."

"Tell me," she pleaded. "I've tried everything I can think of."

"You know a house in the valley beyond

Bright Eyes

Hartfell?" The pony began to explain slowly and carefully. "It stands by a river. A large wheel turns in the water."

"That's the Old Mill," Krista said. "The wheel used to drive an engine for grinding wheat and turning it into flour."

"By the house there is a small field. A pony lives there."

"A chestnut pony? His name's Woody. He belongs to Holly Owen. Her mum and dad own the Old Mill."

"Woody lives there alone. No other ponies visit the valley. Often he is lonely."

Krista nodded slowly. "I heard that Holly gave up riding him last year. I guess he just stands out in the field, not doing much."

"So why not take Alice to see little Woody?" Shining Star suggested. "If she loves ponies, as I think she does, her heart will warm to him."

"It hasn't so far," she argued. There was no magic in Star's plan, and Krista was disappointed. "She's met Misty and all the other ponies at Hartfell, and she's still as sad as anything!"

Once more Shining Star lowered his head to look directly into Krista's eyes. "Trust me," he said. He began to fade back into the silver cloud, to rise above the ground and melt from view.

OK, so there was no magic, no thrill of flying, no wonderful wings beating and rising into the sky. But Krista knew that Star was wise.

"I'll try it," she agreed.

"Good," Shining Star said as he disappeared into the sky. "Take Alice to the Old Mill. See what happens."

Chapter Four

"Misty is really good for jumping," Krista told Alice. "Do you want to try?"

They were in the arena at Hartfell, the morning after Krista had talked with Shining Star.

Alice nodded briefly, so Krista dismounted from Shandy and set up a couple of low jumps. One was a cross-pole, the other a simple parallel bar. "Ready?" she asked.

She stood back as Alice set Misty at the cross-poles and soared over. Then Alice turned the nimble pony around and easily cleared the second jump. "Cool!" she called.

Alice leaned forward to pat Misty's neck. There was colour in her cheeks for once, as she asked Krista to raise the poles.

"Go, Misty!" Krista called, watching the gutsy pony jump with ease.

Alice reined her back then trotted up to Krista. "How about you and Shandy?"

"Shandy's not exactly built for jumping," Krista grinned. She put a foot in the stirrup and swung back into the saddle. "Look at her short little legs!"

No need to be rude! Shandy seemed to say. She shook her head and made the bit and bridle jingle.

As if to prove Krista wrong, the sturdy bay flew over the jumps.

Alice smiled at the sight.

How about that! Krista thought. *Alice Henderson can look happy after all!*

As soon as Jo led her group of trail riders towards the arena, however, Alice's smile fell flat.

Bright Eyes

"Hey, you two, are you going to join us?" Jo asked. "We're heading for the beach."

"Is it OK if we hack out by ourselves?" Krista asked, realising that this would be a good chance to put Shining Star's plan into action. "I want to show Alice some of the best bridleways."

"Sure." Jo's answer came quickly. She turned to Alice. "Stick with Krista. I reckon she knows her way around here better than anyone."

So as the big group set off for the cliffs, Krista and Alice turned inland to climb the high fell above the stable yard.

"I never worry about getting lost on Shandy," Krista admitted. "She knows every part of the trail, and besides, with her you could drop your reins and she'd head straight for home, no problem."

"How come?" Alice asked.

"Shandy's always hungry, and she knows where the feed bins are!"

"She's cute," Alice grinned, letting Misty pick her way up the rocky slope.

Once they reached the ridge, Krista stopped to give the ponies a breather. "See those dark specks on the next hillside?" she asked Alice. "They're moorland ponies."

"Wow, neat. Are they wild?"

Krista nodded. "You're not allowed to capture and tame them. Some of them will come and eat treats, though."

Bright Eyes

"Like Shetlands," Alice murmured, her eyes glazing into the faraway look that she often wore. "I love Shelties. Nessie's got some Shetland in her."

Krista nodded and moved on. She didn't want Alice to mope about the past, so she pointed out landmarks and kept on chatting as they went down into the next valley.

"Soon we have to cross a stream," she warned. "Misty doesn't like crossing it, so make sure she doesn't shy away."

Shandy took the stream in her stride, wading knee deep through the fast flowing water. Krista turned to watch Alice and Misty.

"C'mon, girl!" Alice whispered. "Good girl, you can do it!"

My Magical Pony

The nervous pony put one hoof in the water, snorted and backed off.

Alice squeezed her legs against Misty's flanks.

Misty tried again. She was jittery as she stepped into the stream, but her rider urged her on. Soon she was safe on the far bank.

Krista nodded. "We're going to follow the stream," she explained.

"What's that tall building up ahead?" Alice asked.

"An old water mill." Trying to act casual, Krista rode ahead. Inside, she was nervous.

Take Alice to the Old Mill, Shining Star had told her. *See what happens.*

Well, Krista had managed to do it.

Bright Eyes

Alice was relaxed; so far, so good.

"What's this pony doing all by himself?" Alice asked, the second she spotted Woody grazing in his field.

Krista shrugged and pretended not to know.

"He shouldn't be alone," Alice protested, reining Misty back and waiting for the little chestnut pony to come trotting up. "He needs a friend, don't you, boy?"

Woody poked his head over the hedge.

"He's saying hello! Look, Krista, isn't he sweet?"

"He needs a good brush!" Krista murmured, taking in Woody's rough coat and matted mane.

"Doesn't anyone bother with you?"
Alice asked, reaching over the hedge to
scratch the chestnut's nose. "Are you all on
your own?"

Woody sighed and swished his tail.

Krista had to admit that Shining Star's idea
seemed to be working. Alice was definitely

bonding with the glum, neglected little pony.

But they'd reckoned without Woody's owner, Holly, showing up.

"What do *you* want?" a scornful voice demanded.

Alice jumped back from the hedge to see Holly striding down the lane.

"We're saying hi to Woody," Krista explained.

"You didn't give him any treats, did you?" Holly asked crossly. "He's way too fat already!"

That's probably because you don't give him any exercise! Krista said to herself. Out loud, she assured Holly that poor Woody hadn't had any snacks from them.

My Magical Pony

Ignoring Krista, Holly came right up to Alice. "Anyway, who said you could stroke him? You can't know much about horses if you just go up to them and start petting them without the owner's permission!"

Why is she being so horrible? Krista wondered. *What has Alice ever done to her?*

"I know enough to see that your pony hasn't been brushed for weeks!" Alice replied. "Look at his mane – it's all tangled!"

Uh-oh! Krista saw both girls' tempers flare up. *So much for your brilliant idea, Shining Star!*

"You can shut up, Alice Henderson!" There was no stopping Holly now. She shoved her red, angry face right up to Alice's.

"In fact, I've got a better idea — why don't you get out of here away from Whitton, and go right back to where you came from!"

"It all kicked off when Holly shouted at Alice," Krista explained to Jo. She was back in the stable yard with Shandy and Misty after a hairy ride home.

"Alice ran away?" Jo stood, hands on hips. "She vanished and left you to lead Misty home by yourself?"

Krista nodded. "We came back over the moor." It had been hard, but they'd made it. Misty had been good as gold, tagging along after Shandy. "Holly was pretty mean to Alice," she pointed out.

Jo took Misty's reins and led the pony into her stable. "And do you know where Alice went?"

"Nope. She ran in the opposite direction, down the lane towards the main road. I couldn't follow because of the horses."

"I'd better check in with Mrs Henderson," Jo decided, leaving Krista to untack Misty and Shandy. When she came back from making the call, she was shaking her head and frowning. "There's definitely something wrong there," she muttered. "Like, a major, major problem!"

Krista slung a light sweat rug over Misty's back. She was starting to wish she'd never followed Star's advice. "Did Alice get home?"

Bright Eyes

"Oh yeah, she's home all right."

"What then?"

"Apparently the poor kid's in floods of tears. Her mum can't get any sense out of her." Jo sighed and went to run Misty's metal bit under the cold tap. "Alice is ranting on about Holly's pony being neglected ..."

"... Which he is," Krista pointed out. "I reckon that's why Holly came down so heavily on us – she was ashamed of the way Woody looked."

"Anyway, according to Mrs Henderson, Alice jumps from that to wishing she'd never left Nessie behind, and tells her mum that she's not coming to Hartfell any more.

My Magical Pony

 She chucks her hard hat
into a corner and gives
up riding for good."

Krista groaned. "You're
not serious!"

"I am," Jo assured her,
turning off the tap and shaking drops of water
from the bit.

"She's a great rider. She can't do that!"
Krista sighed.

"She just did," Jo insisted. "Her mother's at
her wits' end. And to cap it all, Alice has
made it totally clear that she is not going to
school tomorrow, or the day after that, or, in
fact, ever again!"

Chapter Five

All that evening, Krista told herself that everything would work out fine.

Shining Star knows what he's talking about, she thought. *No way would he give me a plan that ends in this kind of mess!*

But when she arrived in school next morning, her heart sank to see that Alice's desk was empty.

"Has anyone seen Alice Henderson recently?" Mrs Banks asked during registration.

Krista snuck a look at Holly, who blanked her and started chattering to Carrie.

The teacher marked Alice's place in the register with an 'a' for absent.

"It's the case of the vanishing new girl!" Holly scoffed later in the day. She was with her mates, but she made sure that Krista could overhear. "Now you see her – now you don't!"

And she told everyone how Alice had flared up at her for no reason when she'd been out riding with Krista. "I always thought she was weird," she laughed. "Now I know it for certain!"

Krista noticed that Carrie and some of the others looked uneasy. After Holly had gone, Carrie came up to her and asked if Alice was OK.

Bright Eyes

"She's so *not* OK!" Krista shook her head. "Anyway, the reason Alice lost it with Holly yesterday was because she realised that Holly doesn't look after Woody properly."

"Ah, I get it," Carrie said quietly. And she went off to tell the others.

"Don't worry," Krista's dad told her.

By Tuesday morning, the problem with Alice was definitely getting to Krista. "I just said, should I call for her on my way to school," she muttered. "What's wrong with that?"

"Not a thing, except that you talk about it as if you're going to the dentist to have a tooth out."

Krista managed a smile.

"Like your dad said, try not to worry too much." Giving her a hug, her mum glanced out of the kitchen door to see Mrs Henderson pulling up in her silver car. She raised her eyebrows in surprise.

"Trouble?" Krista's dad asked.

"Probably." Krista's mum went out to meet their visitor.

"Is Krista still here?" Alice's mum asked, then, spotting Krista she gave a sigh of relief.

Bright Eyes

"Good. Krista, I'd like you to take this absence note into school with you and give it to Mrs Banks. Do you mind?"

"That's fine," Krista told her, taking the note.

Krista's mum invited Mrs Henderson in and offered her a cup of tea. "Is Alice OK?"

"Far from it. She's refusing to go to school."

Krista's mum nodded. "Krista mentioned it."

Mrs Henderson looked awful, Krista noticed. Her face was pale and she had dark shadows under her eyes.

"I tried to persuade her, but she was in such a state. Then her dad came up with the idea that he should take a few days off work and drive Alice up to Scotland to see her gran, which is what he's done."

"Maybe a quick visit to her gran will help settle her down," Krista's mum suggested. "Hopefully, she'll come back and be much happier about life."

Or even more homesick than before, Krista thought.

"Here's the deal," Krista told Spike early next morning. "The teachers get trained and we get two days' holiday. How cool is that!"

Spike trampled through the leaves that had fallen from the hawthorn hedge.

"OK, so every day is a holiday to you!" Krista grinned. She was in a great mood, looking forward to a day at the stables.

Bright Eyes

"You hedgehogs don't really have to worry about a thing."

For a while she watched him rooting around the hedge bottom, damp with morning dew. "Hog heaven!" she sighed.

The sound of a car driving up the lane drew Krista to the gate. They didn't get many visitors at High Point, especially at this time of day. Her heart sank a little as Mrs Henderson's small silver car came into view. "Mum!" she called, planning to make herself scarce.

"What is it?" Krista's dad appeared at the back door.

"It's Mrs Henderson." Rolling her eyes, Krista squeezed past him to grab her rucksack. "I'm out of here!"

"Your mum's in the shower," her dad muttered. He put on a fixed smile, ready to say hi to their visitor. But when he saw Mrs Henderson's face, his smile faded. "Go get your mother!" he told Krista.

One glance told Krista why. Alice's mum walked towards them in a daze. She stumbled, as if her legs could hardly hold her up.

Krista's dad went to help. "What's wrong?" he asked, gently leading Mrs Henderson into the house.

Bright Eyes

"It's Alice!" she gasped in a choked voice.

Halfway up the stairs, Krista stopped and held her breath.

"Is she sick?" her dad asked. "Has she had an accident?"

There was a long silence. Krista's mum came out of the bathroom in her dressing gown, her wet hair wrapped in a towel. Krista put a finger to her mouth to warn her to be quiet.

"My husband just called me from his mother's house," Mrs Henderson sobbed. "I didn't know who to come to for help. Something terrible has happened! It was the middle of the night. Everyone was asleep. My husband, Gordon, thought he heard a noise.

He got up and went to Alice's room …" She sobbed loudly.

Krista felt her heart hammering.

At last Mrs Henderson grew calmer. "Gordon went in and turned on the light," she whispered. "The bed was empty. Alice had run away!"

Chapter Six

The moment Krista reached the magic spot, Shining Star appeared.

He flew down the hillside in his cloud of silvery mist, soaring through the air on his wide, white wings.

"There is no time to lose," he told her.

"You know about Alice?" Krista asked. In the confusion at her house, she had slipped away and headed straight to the top of the cliff.

"She is lost."

"She ran away!"

"Yes, and now she is lost," Shining Star insisted. "She is in danger."

Krista closed her eyes and groaned.

"It is not too late," the magical pony said. "But we must make haste. We will journey to a land of lochs and mountains." He had a far-off look, seeming to see the country he spoke of. "There are forests of tall trees, a white river, a great shining lake."

"Can you see Alice? Do you know where she is?" Krista asked urgently. She climbed on to Star's back, ready to fly.

"I see a small house, an empty bed. The girl with red hair has crept away."

Krista took firm hold of the pony's long

mane. "We have to look for her. But where do we start?"

"At the beginning." Shining Star spread his wings. As he gently flapped them, a warm wind surrounded them. "The child vanished in the middle of the night. That is where we will start our search."

"That's impossible!" Krista cried. She held tight as they rose above the cliff. "How can we travel back in time?"

"In Galishe we travel through days and nights," Star explained. "Our ride will take us wherever and whenever we wish to go."

Krista sat astride his back in disbelief. They had never crossed the barrier of time before, and she felt afraid. But if Shining Star had the power to do it, she understood that the best plan would be to return to the moment when Alice had fled.

"We will fly faster than the speed of light," he promised. "You will see this morning's sun rise in the east, you will see last night's stars."

Preparing herself, Krista felt the wind grow stronger and start to whirl. They flew high in the sky, into the clouds. Below them, Whitton Bay and the headland at Black Point disappeared. Then the clouds seemed to wrap themselves around the travellers and form a white tunnel through which Krista and Shining Star flew. The pony shimmered silver, his mane glittered with silver and his wings beat strongly.

My Magical Pony

They flew into the sunrise. Every cloud
was tipped with pink, the sun was a splendid
golden disc. Then the light began to fade.
Ahead of them, at the far end of the whirling
tunnel of mist, was the pale moon.

"Cool!" Krista sighed. Words failed her.
It was beautiful, magical, scary, unbelievable –
a whole mixture of things.

"Look down," Star said.

The moon shone on a world that was
asleep. Tiny lights twinkled along the
motorways like jewels in a necklace; a
city glowed orange. Then they flew over
ghostly-grey mountains and dark forests.
Krista made out the glint of a river that
wound its way across the land, more hills,

a lake as smooth and silver as a mirror.

"How long now?" she asked, feeling the wind tear at her clothes and hair.

"Not long," Shining Star promised. He swooped down towards the ground, tilting sideways and flying in a wide circle over a range of rugged hills surrounding a long, narrow lake.

We must be in Scotland! Krista thought. She saw an island in the middle of the lake, and on the island a ruined castle.

Star hovered overhead then beat his wings to take them towards the far shore of the loch, where a cluster of lights twinkled. "The name of this place is Dunnock," he told Krista. "And here is the house of your friend."

My Magical Pony

Now they were flying over a small town nestled against the water's edge. Boats were moored to a wooden jetty. A single street ran between a huddle of low, stone houses.

"Which one is Alice's gran's?" she asked. "Is it the pink one with the tiny garden?"

"Yes, where the light is on and there is movement," the magical pony replied. He landed on the short jetty and waited for Krista to dismount.

Bright Eyes

She slid from his back. Her legs felt unsteady after the magical journey and her feet sounded hollow on the wooden boards. Ahead she could see the pink bungalow with shadowy figures at the windows.

Shining Star led the way. He stepped from the jetty on to the street then came to a halt. He seemed to be listening.

Krista stopped by his side. She heard the sound of a man's voice from inside the house, then the front door opened suddenly and he appeared, calling Alice's name.

As he came down the short garden path, Shining Star and Krista retreated to the far side of the jetty where they hid.

"Alice!" Mr Henderson called again.

"We're too late. She's already run away!" Krista gasped.

A light in the neighbouring house was switched on, and then another in the cottage beyond that.

"Gordon, come back inside!" an old woman's voice pleaded. "I've found a note in the kitchen. She's run away!"

"We're too late to see where she went," Krista groaned.

Shining Star said nothing. He kept in the shadows and listened.

"Come inside. We must call the police!" the old woman decided.

"Alice, if you're out there hiding, please come back!" Gordon Henderson stood at the gate, staring out into the dark night. "I know you're upset, but we'll try to sort things out, I promise!"

In the shade of the jetty, with the water lapping gently at their feet, Krista shook her head. How desperate Alice must have been to run away like this!

"You'll make your gran ill!" Alice's dad pleaded, stepping out on to the street and staring up the steep hill. Beyond the lights of the village there seemed to be nothing but thick night.

Krista found herself beginning to tremble and put her arm around Star's neck. "Is Alice close by?" she whispered.

He shook his head. "She is already far away."

"Come back!" Mr Henderson cried.

My Magical Pony

A neighbour had emerged on to her doorstep. A man from the pub opposite had opened his bedroom window and leaned out. Soon other voices were calling out.

"It's the wee girl … Aye, the red-head … Gone from her bed!"

Krista shuddered. Shining Star flicked his ears and looked through the darkness on to the heather-covered hillside.

"We'll find her!" Krista vowed under her breath. She was afraid of the dark land and the deep water, but she had Shining Star at her side. "Don't worry, Alice, we'll find you!" she said again.

Her voice was faint and small under the stars.

Chapter Seven

"Come!" Shining Star said to Krista.

She climbed on his back and they waited until the people of Dunnock had closed their doors and the street was quiet once more.

"Where are we going now?" Krista asked, preparing herself for another flight through the night sky.

"To find the girl," Shining Star told her.

They set off on foot along the village street, between the low stone houses. Then the magical pony turned into a lane which took them up a steep hillside.

He seemed to be listening intently and choosing his way carefully.

Krista looked eagerly in every direction. Behind them she could see the winding village street and the smooth surface of the loch reflecting the moon and silvery clouds. To either side was a big expanse of rough moorland. Ahead was a craggy horizon.

With so much space and darkness around them, Krista felt afraid. "Are you sure that Alice came this way?" she asked Star.

The pony stopped, head raised, ears pricked. "She ran from the house and up the hill," he replied. "But I think she turned back before she reached the top."

"Maybe she got lost." *If I'm scared, with*

Bright Eyes

Shining Star to lead me, imagine how frightened Alice must have been! she thought. Small creatures rustled through the heather, an owl flew overhead and was swept off course by a sudden gust of wind.

"I see another pony," Shining Star went on quietly.

The words made Krista jump. She glanced over her shoulder, then up the hill. "Where?" she cried.

"Not here. In a stable nearby. The pony is a dappled grey. She has the look of a high-spirited creature who likes to gallop and be free."

Krista gasped. "That sounds like Nessie – the pony that Alice looked after when she lived up here!"

My Magical Pony

"She loves her dearly. Her heart was broken when they parted."

"I see what she's done!" Krista grew excited. "Alice ran away so she could visit Nessie. She would be longing to see her, but her dad must have said no. So she went to bed and pretended to fall asleep. But as soon as the grown ups went to their bedrooms, she crept out of the house!"

Shining Star nodded. "Do you know where the grey pony lives?" he asked.

Krista frowned. She thought hard, but couldn't remember if Alice had told her anything about the stable yard where she used to help out. And she was beginning to shiver in the cold wind blowing across the

high, open hill.
"She never told me
the name of the stables,"
she had to confess.

Shining Star turned so that their
backs were to the wind. "She is on foot,"
he pointed out. "The place cannot be far."

"But there's nothing around here." As far as
the eye could see, there was only heather and
rocks.

Star decided that they would go back,
cutting across the hillside. They passed
through a dark plantation of pine trees where
the shadows were thick and the pine needles
deadened the pony's footfall.

Krista held tight to his mane.

Beyond the wood was a small farmhouse, guarded by a sharp-eared dog. The dog barked fiercely, so Shining Star carried Krista in a wide loop around the back of the farm.

"Shouldn't we fly?" she asked. That way they could cover the ground more quickly and get a better view.

Star agreed. He beat his wings and they rose in a silver cloud, just high enough to be able to skim the treetops, floating on the air currents like the owl they had seen earlier.

Krista tingled with excitement as they rose above the trees. The magic of flying made her heart beat faster – it was a beautiful, soaring sensation, a freedom like no other.

"There's another farm!" She pointed to a

low building perched by the edge of the loch.

Star flew closer but they soon discovered
that there were no outbuildings large enough
to keep horses in.

Krista thought again – this time about
what Alice's mother had told her and Jo.
"It has to be bigger," she decided. "I know
Alice helped with the mucking out and
getting the horses ready for treks. We need
to find a big house with a stable yard for lots
of horses, not a tiny place like this."

So Shining Star flew on. Krista scanned
the dark hillsides and the border of the
loch, aware of the strong beat of Star's
wings and the flutter of white feathers over
her head.

My Magical Pony

When they came to a place where the heather stopped and bare rock took over, Shining Star rose higher in the sky. He carried Krista over a rocky ridge then dipped down into a green valley which until now had been hidden from sight.

This is better! she thought. Surely here

there would be enough space and plenty of grazing for horses.

Sure enough, there was a large, old house sitting in the valley bottom. Krista made out a square building with a round tower at each corner. The house was surrounded by lawns and gardens. At the back there was a square courtyard overlooked by neat, well-kept stables.

"Shining Star, look down there!" she whispered. "This could be it!"

Star swooped down while Krista hung on. They hovered over the house, noting the ivy that grew up the walls and wound itself around the towers. The windows were long and narrow, the main entrance wide and shaped like a church doorway.

"Spooky!" Krista whispered, picturing long corridors with creaky floorboards, dusty attics and dark cellars.

Shining Star circled overhead then landed by a front gate which had a sign nailed to it.

"Glenmore Lodge and Stables," Krista read, her eyes straining to make out the words in the darkness. "I reckon this is the place!"

"We must go carefully now," Shining Star warned, checking that the house was dark and silent. He led Krista around the side of Glenmore Lodge, through a cluster of silver birch trees to the stable yard at the back.

Krista and Shining Star tried not to make any noise. Even so, the horses in the stables picked up their presence. One whinnied then thrust its head over the stable door. Another turned restlessly on its straw bed.

The magical pony walked quietly up to the edgy chestnut mare who had poked her head over the door. He nudged her with his soft white nose, calming her. Meanwhile, Krista went on down the row.

Each door had a name-plate. She passed an enormous black and white shire horse called Major, then a light bay cob called Whisky. Both were friendly and inquisitive. She patted them in turn then moved on, passing a securely locked barn door, and began to look in the second row of stables. Krista read the sign on the first door – Rosie.

Inside, a cute little Shetland sleepily raised her tousled head.

Krista would have stayed to stroke Rosie, but Shining Star called her from the next stable. "Who lives here?" he asked.

"Highland Lassie." Krista read an old nameplate that had begun to peel and fade. Then she looked into the stable. "Actually, no one," she corrected herself. "It's empty."

"Try the door," Star told her, craning his head to see into the darkest corners.

Krista pulled on the door. It swung open. As she stepped inside, she saw droppings in the straw – a sign that until recently the stable had been occupied like all the rest.

"So where is Highland Lassie?" Shining

Bright Eyes

Star asked, cocking his head. "I think we have a mystery here which might lead us to the red-haired girl."

"But this isn't Alice's old pony," Krista objected. "Her name's Nessie, not Highland Lassie."

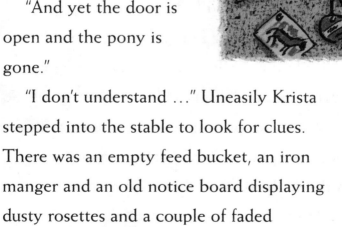

"And yet the door is open and the pony is gone."

"I don't understand …" Uneasily Krista stepped into the stable to look for clues. There was an empty feed bucket, an iron manger and an old notice board displaying dusty rosettes and a couple of faded photographs.

My Magical Pony

One of the photos caught Krista's attention. She could hardly make it out, but there was enough light from the moon to see a grey pony carrying a young rider, both facing the camera. Krista unpinned the picture and took it to Shining Star, turning it over to see a few words scrawled on the back. "'Me and Highland Lassie'," she read.

With trembling fingers Krista turned the photo face up. She studied the face of the rider. Then she gasped. Under the peak of the hard hat was someone she recognised without a shadow of a doubt. It was the smiling face of Alice Henderson.

Chapter Eight

Krista racked her brains, trying to recall every last detail that Alice had told her.

"... I rode a pony called Nessie ... That wasn't her real name."

"Oh, I get it!" Krista gasped. Alice had joked that the pony could be a little terror, so she'd nicknamed her Nessie after the Loch Ness monster. "Highland Lassie is Nessie – they're one and the same pony!"

Shining Star nodded. "We have come to the right place."

"But we're too late – again!" With a sudden

shock, Krista realised that Alice had come to Glenmore with a different plan in mind, and a more drastic one than Krista had expected. "She didn't just want to visit Nessie – she planned to run away with her!"

Shining Star agreed. "A girl who is so unhappy will do dangerous things."

"But where will she go? What will she do?"

"She does not care, as long as she can stay with the pony," Star pointed out. "Her joy at seeing Nessie was so great that she couldn't bear to be parted from her again."

"It's scary!" Krista sighed, glancing towards the huge house. "What's going to happen?"

"The girl's father will have the whole village out looking for his daughter," Star said.

Bright Eyes

"I suppose that Alice will ride the pony far away, hoping not to be discovered."

"Then we have to follow her and find her before they do," Krista decided. "She might listen to me."

"So much sadness," Shining Star said, shaking his head. Then he told Krista to sit on his back. "We must look for prints on the ground," he decided. "That way we can find out which direction the girl and the pony took."

So, in the pearly grey light of the approaching dawn, Krista and Shining Star searched carefully in the grounds of Glenmore Lodge.

They went between the birch trees,

a silvery-white horse and a serious-looking, dark-haired girl, scanning the ground for hoof-prints.

"The grass is churned up by other horses," Krista sighed. "How can we tell which ones belong to Nessie?"

Bright Eyes

"These are dried out and old. Nessie's will be fresh," Star pointed out. He took Krista beyond the grounds of the lodge, stopping by a narrow stream and examining the soft banks.

"If Alice and Nessie crossed the stream, that would mean they were heading for the shore of the lake," Krista said. She gazed into the distance, beyond the island with the ruined castle, at the still water and the sheer, grey rocks rising from it. "I wonder if they know a hidden track where no one could follow."

"Look there, in the mud!" Shining Star drew Krista's attention back to the ground beneath their feet.

She followed the direction of the magical pony's gaze, and there, a few metres upstream, was a freshly disturbed patch of ground.

Krista dismounted and stooped to examine it. "Definitely hoof marks," she reported. "And they're pony-size!"

"Here is hair from the pony's tail," Star said. He stood beside a thorn bush where long, dark grey hairs had become entangled.

"They're the right colour!" Krista exclaimed, gasping again when she found a shiny blue and silver object half-covered by water. "Look, here's a torch!"

"The girl must have dropped it as they crossed the water." Star lowered his head to take in the scents of the pony and girl who had come this way.

"It looks like they had a struggle to cross." Krista pointed to the areas where the pony's feet had sunk deep into the mud. "Maybe Nessie reared up and Alice almost lost her balance. That's when the torch dropped out of her hand. But see – the track carries on!"

Sure enough, there was a trail leading up a hill towards a rocky outcrop. While Star stepped through the fast running water, Krista jumped from rock to rock, keeping her feet dry and landing beside him. She went on foot up the hill until they reached the top and she found that they were overlooking the village once more.

My Magical Pony

"Hmm." Krista hadn't expected Alice to be riding Nessie towards Dunnock. "I would've thought she'd keep away from people's houses. Instead, she seems to want to be seen!"

But Shining Star shook his head. "The hoof-prints tell me that the pony came up the hill at a gallop, as if in fear."

"You mean, he reared up in the mud by the stream and then ran away with his rider?" Krista frowned at the idea of Nessie bolting. Yet Alice had admitted that the grey pony was a handful.

Deep in thought, Star and Krista looked down on the waking village. In the east the sun was rising, throwing a pink glow over the loch.

"So what now?" Krista asked. She'd lost the trail once it had reached the open, rocky space on which they stood.

Down in the next valley Shining Star saw a light go on in one of the houses, then another. He picked out the pink walls of old Mrs Henderson's house, noticing the curtains being drawn back.

"We're getting nowhere!" Krista groaned, her shoulders sagging. Even though Shining Star had performed his magic and flown back through the night, morning had come and they were not a single step nearer to finding poor, runaway Alice.

"We go on!" Star said firmly. He raised his head, and his dark eyes widened as if they could see the future.

Chapter Nine

"We go on!" Star had said.

But, without a trail to follow, Krista couldn't see how they could possibly find Alice and Nessie.

"It's about now that Mr Henderson will be calling Mrs Henderson and telling her the bad news," she realised. Time had caught up with Shining Star. The day had begun with a pink dawn, but soon turned cold and grey.

"The pony was afraid and galloped up the hill," Star insisted. He turned to Krista. "Is the girl a good rider?"

Bright Eyes

Krista nodded. "Excellent. Even Jo was impressed."

"So let us suppose that she stayed in the saddle and brought Nessie under control. Then I think she would have turned back from the village and cut down the hill, taking care to keep out of sight of Glenmore."

"Let's try," Krista agreed, on the lookout for fresh prints as they descended into a stony valley. "This isn't good," she mumbled, feeling the sides of valley close in on them. "I can't see any hoof-prints. And in any case, it comes to a dead end."

Shining Star took in every detail – the hillsides covered in loose, flat stones, the bare horizons. He inspected a trickle of water running over mossy rocks, walked on a little way then stopped. "There is no life here," he said calmly. "We must turn around."

Krista sighed. They had lost precious time.

As they turned to retrace their steps, Shining Star heard a distant sound. He broke into a trot, his hooves clattering over the stones.

Krista held on, listening but hearing nothing unusual.

"It was a pony calling," Star told her, breaking out of the narrow valley on to a narrow band of grass and reeds bordering the loch. He set off at a gallop over the smooth ground.

Krista crouched low, feeling the wet mist

on her face. She had heard nothing except the wind, but she trusted the magical pony's word. "Can you hear it now?" she demanded.

"Yes," he told her. "We are drawing near."

They galloped along the water's edge, sometimes splashing through streams, then swerving past trees. Krista ducked to avoid the branches, her heart pounding. Only when they came to a fence did Star slow down.

Beyond the high fence was an old house surrounded by trees, with a rickety boathouse and a jetty leading out into the lake.

"Listen!" Star warned.

And this time Krista heard the shrill call of a horse in trouble. It came from the pebble beach beyond the jetty – a long, high whinny accompanied by the clatter of hooves on the stones.

"It must be Nessie!" Krista exclaimed, ready to run to the pony's aid.

But Shining Star wanted to wait. "I can hear a voice," he warned, turning towards the house.

An old woman stood in the doorway, speaking into her phone. "The pony is trapped," she explained. "She's caught her bridle over a fence post. The more she struggles, the worse it gets. I can't go near ... No, I don't know what happened to the rider. The pony's terrified. Can you come straight away?"

Quickly, without stopping to think, Krista slipped from Shining Star's back and ran towards the woman. "Can I help?" she asked.

"There's a pony down by the loch. She's in a dreadful state." Shaking her head, the woman led Krista down the path to show her. "I've called the RSPCA to free the poor thing."

Krista braced herself as they approached the beach. The trapped pony's shrill whinnies grew louder. Krista saw her and stopped in her tracks.

Poor Nessie had managed to snag her bridle over the pointed top of a wooden post. She'd tugged hard and pulled the post out of the ground, but then the barbed wire attached to it had snapped and caught itself in the pony's mane. Now Nessie couldn't move without feeling a sharp stab of pain from the cruel spikes.

"Every time I go near, she panics," the lady explained. "She's been there at least half an hour, poor thing."

"Let me try," Krista said, glancing back at Star, who stood by the gate.

Bright Eyes

The old lady spotted only a common grey moorland pony and not the magical flying creature that Krista could see. "So you know about horses?" she asked.

Krista nodded and moved closer to the terrified Nessie. The pony's eyes rolled with fear, her nostrils were wide and her ears laid flat against her head.

"Take care!" the woman pleaded.

"Easy!" Krista murmured. This was definitely Nessie, but where on earth was Alice?

Nessie pulled harder at the post as Krista drew near. She tried to rear, but the barbed wire pressed against her neck.

"Easy!" Krista insisted, using her voice to

try and calm the pony. "Pulling only makes it worse. If you let me near, I can help you!"

The pony breathed hard. Every muscle in her body was tense. But she stopped struggling as Krista approached.

"Good girl!" Krista laid a hand on Nessie's hot neck then worked her fingers up towards the bridle. She wanted to unhook the strap that was caught on the fence post, but she had to take care to avoid the strand of barbed wire. And she must keep the pony calm.

"Do be careful!" the old lady murmured.

Shining Star watched patiently.

Sweating and breathing noisily, nevertheless Nessie allowed Krista to unhitch the bridle.

"Stand!" Krista warned. Even though she

had freed the bridle, the wire was still entangled in Nessie's mane. Now she must work at the strands of hair and pray that the pony stayed still.

Back on the road, a white van drew up and a uniformed man and woman got out. The owner of the house rushed to meet the two RSPCA officers.

Krista worked on. Slowly she untangled Nessie's mane. "You're so good!" she whispered to the pony. "Brave girl, we're almost finished!"

Nessie trembled. The barbed wire had made tiny cuts on her neck which were trickling blood. The poor pony was exhausted by her struggle.

My Magical Pony

At last Krista was able to separate the last strand of hair and lead Nessie away from the fence.

"Nice work." The female RSPCA officer came forward. She smiled at Krista. "You handled that very well."

Krista thanked her. "We were just passing."

The woman took Nessie's reins. "This pony comes from Glenmore stable yard – we already had a call from the police telling us she was missing. Apparently it's linked with the disappearance of a kid from a house in Dunnock."

Krista thought it was best to say nothing, so she shrugged and made off towards Shining Star.

Bright Eyes

"Hey, what's your name?" the woman officer called. "Why don't you stick around? I'm sure the Glenmore people would like to thank you."

"No, we've got to go," Krista said hurriedly. No way did she want to be here when the police arrived. Once they started asking questions, she and Star would never get away. "I'm glad the pony's OK though."

"Well, thanks for what you did," she said with a nod and a grin. "We'll take over from here – get the pony back to her yard, have her cleaned up and looked after."

Krista smiled back.

"Maybe I'll visit her later."

"Yeah, do that." With a friendly wave the woman saw Krista and Shining Star on their way.

Star leaned his head towards Krista. "You did well," he told her. "But now we must hurry."

Krista glanced back at the scene. The man from the RSPCA was easing a sweat-blanket over Nessie's back, while the woman checked her cuts.

"How could Alice run off and leave Nessie trapped like that?" Krista exclaimed, walking quickly to catch up with Star. "How could she be so cruel?"

Shining Star walked on, listening and

Bright Eyes

watching. "I don't think she did run off," he said after a long pause.

Krista ran beside him until they were out of sight of the house. "Meaning what?" she cried. She felt an urgency in Shining Star's manner, and it worried her. "If Alice didn't panic and run away when Nessie got caught up in the barbed wire, what on earth *did* happen?"

Chapter Ten

"I believe the red-haired girl is in serious trouble," Shining Star told Krista.

He had told her to climb on his back and was spreading his wings for flight. "I listen and I hear only silence. I look across the hillsides and I see no movement."

"But Alice has to be out there!" Krista insisted. "She got this far, at least!"

Shining Star began to beat his wings. "No," he argued. "All we can be sure of is that the grey pony reached the spot by the lake. It seems to me now that the girl did not."

Bright Eyes

Krista held on as they rose above the ground, higher than the beech trees that bordered the road. "How come they were separated?" she asked shakily.

"Suppose the girl was thrown from the saddle and is lying injured." Star soared over the trees, tilting his wings so that they changed course and flew back the way they had come. "Even an excellent rider can be taken by surprise. If a horse suddenly bucks or rears, there is little anyone can do."

Krista knew this was true. And an accident like this could explain why they'd found poor Nessie alone and trapped. Her thoughts whirled as they flew higher and faster.

Below them, the countryside opened up to moorland and rocky hills. Way in the distance, the loch shimmered with a cold, grey sheen. "There's so much ground to cover!" she sighed.

Shining Star flew swiftly. Swooping close to the heathery hillside, he hovered by a stream which splashed over boulders in a tumbling waterfall. He pointed out hoof-prints to Krista.

"They're too big for Nessie," she said with a shake of her head.

Still retracing their steps, convinced that Alice had been hurt in an accident, Star flew over Glenmore Lodge.

Between his beating wings, Krista caught

glimpses of the ivy-covered house. She saw people like matchstick men in the stable yard, a miniature police car parked by the gate. She knew that Star's magic prevented them from seeing him flying.

Unreal! she thought, as they flew on.

Star circled again and flew over the village. Here again there was a great deal of activity – people gathered in the street outside the pink house and more police cars.

Star flew slowly from the village, over the hill to Glenmore once more. He found the place where Alice had dropped her torch and hovered again. "Ah!" he said softly.

"Ah … what?" Krista saw his ears prick. He seemed suddenly alert.

"I believe I made a mistake." With a rapid beat of his wings, he followed the old trail of hoof-prints to the top of the hill, where he landed, gazing down into the bare, steep-sided valley with the stream running through it.

"We looked here before!" Krista protested. It was the dead valley, full of stones and rocks. "You said there was no life here."

"I was wrong." Star walked slowly over the loose grey rocks, his hooves sounding hollow, his breath rising as a silvery mist. "True, it is silent."

And how! Krista shuddered.

"… But there may be life after all."

Krista felt Shining Star sway then stumble.

Bright Eyes

She began to listen and to search every dark shadow between the rocks. All at once, she got a sense that the magical pony was right – that the narrow valley wasn't deserted after all.

She held her breath, trying not to let fear seize her. They disturbed a big, black rook, which flapped its wings and rose into the air. Then a grey rabbit bolted out of a crevice and fled towards the stream.

"Alice?" Krista said. Her voice sounded tiny and muffled.

"She can't hear you," Star warned, stepping

firmly on. "She's here, but it's no use calling her."

"Are you sure?" Krista couldn't help it – the fear came rushing at her and grabbed her by the throat until she could hardly breathe.

"She's here," the magical pony said again.

And in one of the deep shadows, under an overhanging rock, Shining Star and Krista found Alice.

The magical pony stopped by the rock. Krista leaned down and looked under the overhang. She saw something blue, then a streak of reddish-brown. Alice was lying on her stomach, her hair covering her face, one arm flung wide. She didn't move.

"Is she dead?" Krista gasped.

"Alive," Shining Star insisted. "Her breath is

shallow. Her mind is lost in dreams."

"She must be unconscious!" Krista felt the panic rising. "Should I try to move her?"

"No. Fetch water from the stream. Scoop it between your hands and carry it carefully."

Krista ran to do as she was told, trying not to spill the precious water as she returned. Shining Star stood guard over the girl.

"Alice, wake up!" Krista urged. She stooped beside the body, offering the water she had brought.

"Sprinkle a little over her cheek," Star said.

Krista sighed. What if Alice never moved again? What if she didn't wake up? Carefully she released a few drops.

Alice stirred. She took a deep breath.

"More!" Shining Star urged.

Krista gently moved Alice's hair to one side and sprinkled a few more drops. It seemed an age, but at last Alice moved again and her eyes flickered open.

"It's me – Krista!"

The dull, grey-green eyes blinked then opened again. Alice struggled to turn over on to her back. "Where am I?"

Krista helped her to sit up. "It's OK, you're safe!"

"I'm cold! Where's Nessie?" Alice's eyes were full of dread as she recalled her accident.

"Nessie's safe too." Krista took off her jacket and wrapped it around Alice's shoulders. "Do you want to tell us what happened?"

Bright Eyes

"Nessie spooked. I think it was a fox." As Alice's blurred memory cleared, she rushed to tell Krista the whole story. "Something shot out from under this rock. Nessie reared and threw me off. That's the last I remember."

"You were unconscious. But you're OK now?" Krista checked. It didn't seem as if Alice had broken any bones in her fall.

Gradually a warm feeling of relief passed through her. She glanced up at Shining Star, who nodded.

"I want to see Nessie!" Alice insisted.

Krista frowned. "I don't know if you can right now."

"Why not? She's OK, isn't she? You said she was!"

"Yes, she got caught up in some barbed wire, but she's not badly hurt. The RSPCA came."

"Oh, poor thing!" Alice looked horrified. "It's all my fault! I shouldn't have taken her out at night!"

"Look, calm down." Krista didn't want Alice to stand up, but she couldn't prevent her.

Bright Eyes

Alice looked frantically up and down the narrow valley. "I missed Nessie so much and only wanted to ride her one more time. I thought I could get her back to the stables before morning and no one would ever know!"

"I get it," Krista assured her. "But you didn't think it through."

"It all went wrong," Alice cried. She covered her face with her hands.

Helplessly Krista glanced at Shining Star.

"Tell her to climb up," he said quietly.

"Listen, Star will carry you back to the village," Krista explained. "Your dad and gran need to know you're safe."

With a sob, Alice accepted a leg up on to Shining Star's back.

My Magical Pony

"Can you ride bareback?" Krista checked.

When Alice nodded, she gave the magical pony the signal to set off. Slowly the three of them made their way out of the grim valley.

"It all went horribly wrong!" Alice said again.

Krista frowned. She pictured the police, the RSPCA, the owner of Glenmore, all wanting to quiz the runaway. Alice might be safe, but it wasn't over yet – not by a long way!

Chapter Eleven

"All will be well," Shining Star told Krista quietly.

He had carried Alice all the way to the village and set her down outside her gran's house.

Krista crossed her fingers and watched the scared girl make her way up the path. Alice knocked with a trembling hand at her gran's door.

The door opened slowly. Old Irene Henderson looked out.

For a long moment, neither the girl nor the

old lady spoke. Then Alice's gran held her
arms open.

"It's my precious girl!" she sighed.

Alice's dad was called and he came rushing
back. His pale face broke into a smile the
moment he saw his daughter.

If Alice said "sorry" once, she said it a
hundred times.

"Hush!" her gran told her. "And listen to
me. I took it upon myself to ask your father
and he has agreed to let you take that wee
pony back to Whitton with you."

"Nessie?" Alice gasped.

"I told you all would be well," Shining Star
said contentedly from the pebble beach

where he and Krista quietly watched.

"When are you ever wrong?" Krista smiled.

"I spoke to the people at Glenmore," Gordon Henderson confirmed. "They realise how much the pony means to you and they're willing to sell her to us. Your mum agrees too."

"Wow!" Krista sighed.

Alice's eyes opened wide as she looked from her gran to her dad and back again. "Do you mean it?" she gasped.

"Look – look at her eyes," Star murmured.

Krista had to wait until Alice turned round. Then, from their quiet spot by the jetty, she could see what Shining Star meant.

Alice's face was lit up with an expression

that she'd never seen before. It transformed her pale features and made her into a new, happy person.

"Her eyes are sparkling!" Krista said.

"Like emeralds," the magical pony agreed. "Our job is done. Now we must fly home."

"Guess what, Shining Star – Woody has come to live at Hartfell too!"

Krista stood on the magic spot. It was a week since her magical pony had flown her back from Scotland, three days since little Nessie had arrived at Jo Weston's stables. Now Krista wanted to pass on some more great news.

"Star, are you there?" she asked.

Bright Eyes

A warm wind blew across the cliff-top.
There seemed to be a silver glitter in the air.

"OK, you're here. Are you ready to listen?"
Krista went on. "I just left Woody and Nessie
with Alice in the top field. They're getting on
great together. Jo decided she needed another
pony for trail rides, so Alice told her about
Woody at the Old Mill, and Jo went to see
him and said he would be perfect. She bought
him from the Owens on the spot. Isn't that
cool?"

The silver mist wafted against Krista's
smiling face. She knew that her magical pony
had heard every word she said.

"Yeah, totally cool!" she breathed. "Oh, and
by the way, I told Alice not to say a word

My Magical Pony

about us being up there in Scotland. She did
ask me, how come we'd arrived? But I went
kind of vague and said it was a secret – that

Bright Eyes

you were a special pony and not to ask any more questions. Alice was fine about it."

Krista leaned back her head and breathed in the presence of Shining Star.

"Krista!" An excited Alice called from further along the cliff path. "Come and see Nessie making friends with Misty and Shandy. It's really sweet!"

Krista grinned then nodded. "Bye!" she told her magical pony. "I'm wanted by the girl with sparkling eyes!"

Slowly the silver mist lifted and Krista ran down the path to join Alice.